Megan Flanner

I Can Read Books
with
Rhyming Riddles

BOOK 2

This book belongs to

_____

 # Dear_____!

 # Find
the answer
on the
next page

I am furry, and I love to play,

I bark and my tail wags all day.

I love to go for walks or a jog,

I am a ...

Find the answer on the next page

Dog

I have many pages filled with words,

I can tell you about lots of things

around the world.

Open me up if you want to have

a look,

I am a...

?

Find the answer on the next page

Book

She does a lot for you,

She really loves you.

She is the same to you

And your sister and your brother.

She is your...

Find the answer on the next page

Mother

I live very high in the sky,

So far up, the birds can't

reach me when they fly.

You won't see me in the morning

or at noon,

I am the...

Find the answer on the next page

Moon

You need me when you are hungry,

If you don't get me you will be angry.

If you chew me with your mouth

open, you'll be called rude,

I am...

Find the answer on the next page

Food

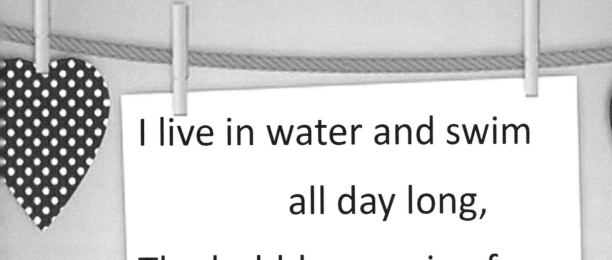

I live in water and swim
all day long,
The bubbles coming from
my mouth are a song.
You keep me in a glass bowl,
I'm a...

Find the answer on the next page

Fish

I like to jump and skip and hop,

If I slip, I might do a belly flop!

I'm green and I live in a bog,

I'm a...

Find the answer on the next page

Frog

It's blue and wet,

In large pools, it collects.

If it's not cold, then it's

a lot hotter.

It's...

Find the answer on the next page

Water

I can touch the Earth and

I can touch the sky,

Thunder follows closely when

I'm nearby.

My sound is loud and frightening.

I am a bolt of...

Find the answer on the next page

Lightning

I am small, white, and I have a gate,

I can surround an entire estate.

Climbing over me wouldn't make

sense,

I am a...

Find the answer on the next page

Fence

Sad, happy, angry, or just

having fun,

You'll see these things in everyone.

I'm the reason your feelings are

always in motion.

I am...

Find the answer on the next page

Emotion

It is lighter than a feather,

It is a part of the weather.

At it, you cannot stare.

It is the...

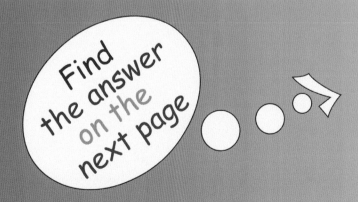

Find the answer on the next page

Air

From one end of the sky

to the other, I stretch,

A pot of gold from my end

you must fetch.

You look up at me from your window,

I am a...

Find the answer on the next page

Rainbow

When I'm gone, it is dark and cold,

I am yellow, and I shine like gold.

When I'm up in the sky, you can

have lots of fun.

I am the...

Find the answer on the next page

Sun

You pick from the ground
so you can smell my head,
The dirt by your feet is my
home and my bed.
I'm small and pretty,
but stand tall like a tower,
I am a...

Find the answer on the next page

Flower

We are small and have

long skinny tails,

We don't like birds and

run faster than snails.

We think your cheese is very nice.

We are...

Find the answer on the next page

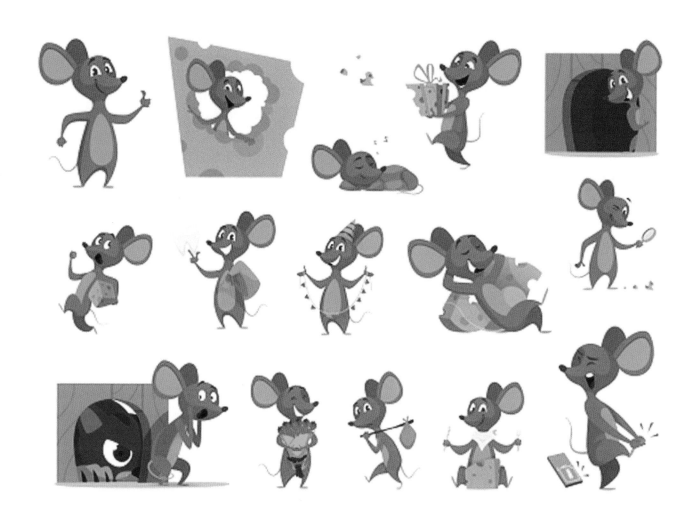

Mice

I grow a fruit that can be

green or red,

They might drop from my

branches and hit your head!

They might taste sweet

to you and a bee,

I am an...

Find the answer on the next page

Apple tree

You can wear it outside,
You can wear it inside.

It has holes for your arms
to fit through the sides.

You may need to wash it
if it falls in the dirt.

It is a...

Find the answer on the next page

Shirt

You can dance or sing along

if you like,

You can listen to me anywhere,

even when riding a bike.

I can be short, or I can be long,

I am a...

Find the answer on the next page

Song

Look into me and you'll see
                    only yourself,
I can be hanging from the wall
                    or a shelf.
Clean me up if you want
                    to see clearer,
I am a...

Find the answer on the next page

Mirror

When you're having fun, I fly by,

You can tell me by using a clock

or the sun in the sky.

When I reach twelve, the clock

will chime,

I am...

Find the answer on the next page

Time

When I fall from the sky, everyone
runs inside,
Those who don't want to get wet
must try and hide.
You can watch me safely from
your windowpane,
I am the...

Find
the answer
on the
next page

Rain

It can be made out of wood

or metal,

The waves make it hard for it

to settle.

On the ocean, you'll see it float,

It is a...

Find the answer on the next page

Boat

It's tiny, cute, and its fur makes
it look fat,
It looks really good when
wearing a hat.
Its worst enemy is a nasty rat.
It is a...

Cat

You can wear it on your head,

It would be silly to wear it

to bed.

It would look good on a cat,

It is a...

Find the answer on the next page

Hat

Find the answer on the next page

I am round and make a noise that wakes people when they're asleep.

If you set me down on a table, then you won't hear a peep.

If you bang me around, then you won't have to yell.

I am a...

Bell

I'm orange and good for

eyesight,

I'm a rabbit's favorite thing

to bite.

My name sounds a lot like *parrot*,

I am a...

Find the answer on the next page

Carrot

Something lays them.

Something sits on them.

They don't have arms or legs.

They are...

Find the answer on the next page

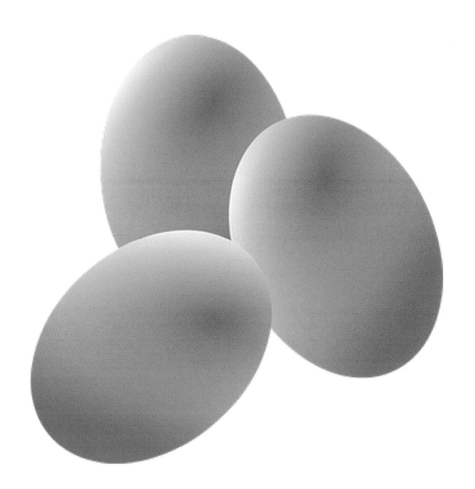

Eggs

Everyone lives in one—

even you do!

It can be big or small with some

windows and a roof.

There's even a tiny one

for a mouse.

It is a...

Find the answer on the next page

House

You always give me things to hold,
I have no choice; I must do as
I'm told.

I am long but I have four legs
to keep me stable,

I am a...

Find the answer on the next page

Table

Some of them sing and
some of them talk.

Some of them fly and
some of them walk.

It has feathers, and its voice
can always be heard.

It is a...

Find the answer on the next page

Bird

I come out at night, only
when the lights are out,
I will show up every time;
there's no need to doubt.
You may want to make a wish or
keep me in a jar,
I am a...

Find the answer on the next page

Star

I am red as fire

With a fluffy tail.

I like long walks.

I am a...

Find the answer on the next page

Fox

When I am here,

flowers don't grow,

and children play in the snow.

What season am I?

Find the answer on the next page !!!

Winter

The END

Thanks for reading my book! If you enjoyed it, please leave an honest review, because I'd love to hear your feedback, thoughts and ideas...
Even if it's just a sentence or two! I read all of your reviews! Your reviews help spread the word to other readers, and they also inspire me to create new books to enjoy.

Thank you so much!!!

I really do appreciate it!

Megan Flannery

Book 1

https://www.amazon.com/dp/B087H7YX6F

Printed in Great Britain
by Amazon